AF595890
Garden of Joy
Heartfelt Home
Mindful Meadow
Giggly Treetops
Bravelands
Forest of Fulfilment
Placid Peak
Positivity Pole
This is young **Sprout,** he's a really fun **guy.**
Flick through the book, it's not hard to see why.
He likes to **pop up** here and there.
Take a look, he's **everywhere!**

**Dedicated to Darcy and Owen.
For being my real-life happy place.**

Scholastic Australia Pty Limited
PO Box 579 Gosford NSW 2250
ABN 11 000 614 577
www.scholastic.com.au

Part of the Scholastic Group
Sydney • Auckland • New York • Toronto • London • Mexico City • New Delhi
Hong Kong • Buenos Aires • Puerto Rico

Published by Scholastic Australia in 2024.

Edited by Charlotte Bachali, Michelle Lee and Hannah Francis | Designed by Alyce Levett

ISBN 978-1-76152-690-9

Printed in China.

Scholastic Australia's policy, in association with its printers, is to use papers that are renewable and made efficiently from wood grown in responsibly managed forests, so as to minimise its environmental footprint.

Scholastic Australia respects and honours Aboriginal and Torres Strait Islander Elders past, present and future. We acknowledge the stories, traditions and living cultures of Aboriginal and Torres Strait Islander peoples on this land and are committed to building a brighter future together.

A catalogue record for this book is available from the National Library of Australia

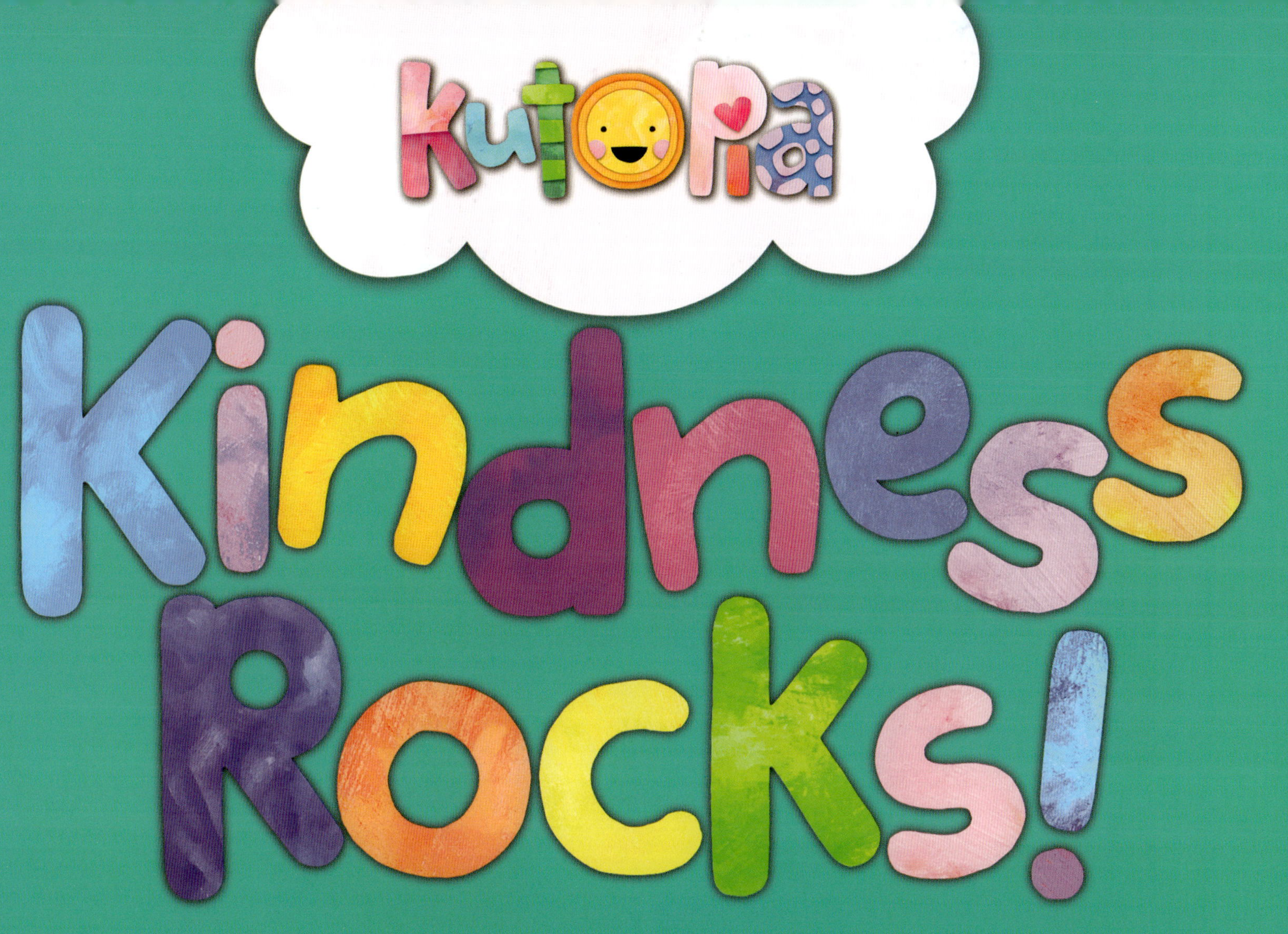

Written & Illustrated by

kasey rainbow

SCHOLASTIC

SYDNEY AUCKLAND NEW YORK TORONTO LONDON MEXICO CITY
NEW DELHI HONG KONG BUENOS AIRES PUERTO RICO

In Kindness Rocks, in the hot morning sun,
sits Leo the Leopard, warming his tum.
He watches the frillies frolic and play,
hoping that maybe he'll join them one day.

Leo spots Frankie on the sideline, alone.
He feels her sadness, as though it's his own.

See, he knows the feeling of being left out.
Then, out of nowhere, he hears a small shout . . .

'Oi!' The voice yells.
'Stop right this minute!'

'That kind thought you're having?
You'd better bin it!'

Leo's confused, what's happening now?
As he thinks, a spot **leaps** off his brow!

'The name's
Meanie Bo Beanie.
How do you do?
Stop.
Don't tell me. I don't care about **you**.

I'm the voice you can hear in your mind.
Leo, you don't know how to be kind!

'You know you don't have the right words to say.
There's just no way you could brighten her day.
So why even bother?
Just leave her alone.
Instead, walk away and play on your own.'

With a sigh, Leo feels the sadness seep in.
Meanie is right . . . where could he begin?
But then, with a flutter he feels in his heart,
brave little Leo knows just
where to start.

Meanie smiles smugly as Leo walks off.
'I told you so,' he says with a scoff.
Meanie thinks he has won, but—just then—
they get to Finn the fennec fox's den.

With a **squeak of joy,** Finn jumps up in surprise.
Then he sees the sadness behind Leo's eyes.
'You're blue!' says Finn. 'Can you tell me why?'
Leo points at the frilly, feeling quite shy.

'You want to help her?' said Finn. 'Ah, I see!
Well Leo, I'm sure glad that you came to me!
If you can't find the words, why not lend an ear?
Because listening says,
"It's okay friend, I'm here".

'Making friends can be hard, but
you're not on your own.
There's a reason why **Kindness Rocks** is our home.
Let's go and see **Miah,** and ask her advice.
She can teach us what it means to be nice.'

As they set off together, Leo's mind squeals,
I wonder if *this* is how kindness *feels?*
With Finn by his side, the sun seems a bit brighter.
And Meanie feels smaller, a little bit lighter.

Finn cares about Leo, makes him feel understood.
Leo learns that asking for help can be **good.**

Miah is known for her kindness and caring,
Leo can't wait for the wise words she'll be sharing!

They spot **Miah the Meerkat,** holding her pup.
Finn is certain his friend can cheer Leo up.

'Hi Miah,' says Finn.

'We're in a bit of a bind.
Leo is struggling with how to be kind.'

'Oh Leo,' she says, 'there's no need to be blue.
There's more to kindness than a sentence or two.
Why not draw a picture?
Paint an artwork to share?
We can use more than words to show that we care.

'Kindness is much more than simply a word.
It's listening to those who long to be heard.

It's a friendly smile, to those with a frown.
It's giving a hug to someone who's down.

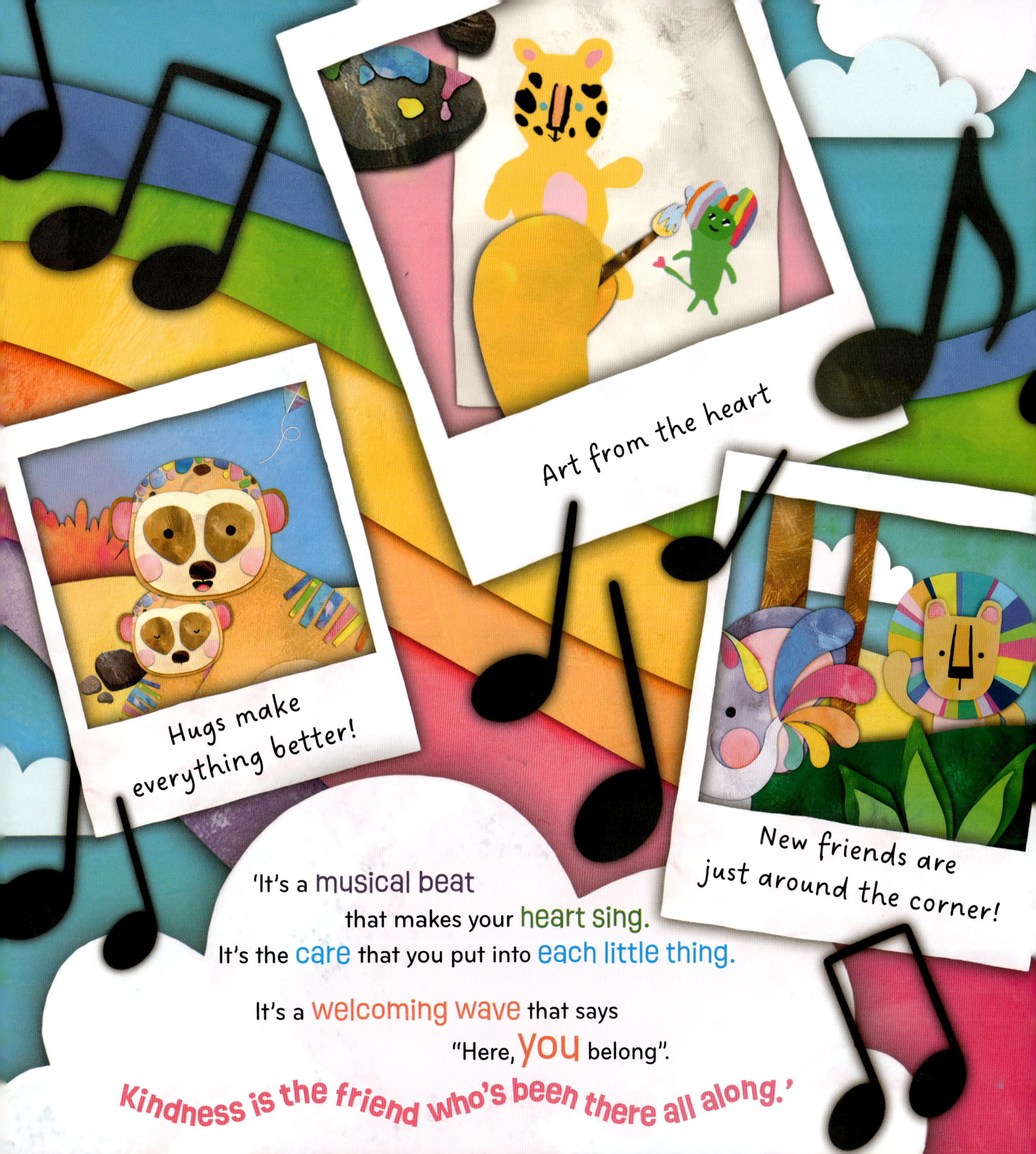

'It's a musical beat
that makes your heart sing.
It's the care that you put into each little thing.

It's a welcoming wave that says
"Here, you belong".
Kindness is the friend who's been there all along.'

With a wave of thanks, Leo turns to run.
Because now he knows what needs to be done.

As Leo hurries, Meanie struggles to stay.
And with one big leap . . .

WHOOSH!

He's blown away.

Back in the rocks, it is quiet and still.
All alone sits the lizard with the **colourful frill.**

As she looks up from her spot on the ground,
she sees Leo waving and feels she's been found.

Leo stands by her side and puts his art on the sand.
It's a picture of them, as they play hand in hand.
She smiles and says, 'Would you like to play?'
Leo holds out his paw, nodding okay.
THE ART OF WARMTH

As they start to play, Leo gives a big grin,
and, as he does, he feels a sparkle within.
Where Meanie once sat, there on his face,
is now a small heart
nestled in place.

From that moment on, Leo paints and he draws
for his friends old and new, with his talented paws.
And each time he gives out a piece of his art,
he feels a warm glow in his new little heart.

The next time you're struggling with the words to be kind,
ignore those mean thoughts inside of your mind.
Remember the importance of kindness, in fact . . .
you can change someone's life with a small, simple act.

A note for readers...

Each land within the whimsical world of Kutopia represents characteristics that we all possess and can continue to build as we learn and grow. Each colourful critter residing within holds their own unique 'special sparkle' and is ready and waiting to take you on a journey to discover these strengths within yourself.

KINDNESS ROCKS

Kindness is wanting to listen, help and understand others, even when you may not get anything in return. Even small acts of kindness can make a huge difference in our own lives and the lives of others.

LEO
Kind

MIAH
Caring

FINN
Compassionate

FRANKIE
Empathetic

Conversation starters:

- What does it mean to be kind?
- How do you feel when someone is kind to you?
- What were some examples of kindness you spotted throughout the book?

Activities!

- Write a note for a friend and pop it in their mailbox as a surprise!
- Paint some rocks from your garden and leave them at a park for someone to find.
- Don't forget to be kind to yourself! Write a list of things you love about you.

nkie
Forever!
Come visit us
@this.is.kutopia on Instagram
and thisiskutopia.com
See more of
Kasey @kasey.rainbow
on Instagram!
A note from the author
Kutopia is more than a tale to unfold,
it is a place to discover the powers you hold.
Once you discover the strengths you possess,
life's struggles will hold you back less and less.

kasey rainbow's
Kutopia
WHEN I GROW UP